C2 03:15

C1 03:17

C7 03:24

C5 03:02

C6 02:41

C3 02:33

C3   02:50

C6   02:41

C2   03:16

C4   03:03

C5   02:51

C8   03:19

For Tiffany, Phil, and Laura with thanks

First
published in
Great Britain 2002
by Egmont Books
L i m i t e d
2 3 9 K e n s i n g t o n
H i g h   S t r e e t
L o n d o n   W 8   6 S A

Text and illustrations copyright
© M i k e B o s t o c k 2 0 0 2
Mike Bostock has asserted his moral rights
D e s i g n   b y   P h i l   P o w e l l
i s b n   1   4 0 5 2   0 0 8 0   4
A CIP catalogue record for this title is available from the British Library

Printed in Singapore

1 3 5 7 9 10 8 6 4 2

BLOOP

Shopping

story and pictures by Mike Bostock

EGMONT

This is Louie.

And this
is Bloop.

Bloop is Louie's cuddliest,
most precious toy.

He is a Thing with a String.
A long wiggly string that goes
BLOOP when Louie pulls it.

Today, Louie and his mum
have been to the supermarket.

The supermarket on Andromeda 9
on the far side of the Alpha Galaxy.

They have bought everything they need to make Louie's favourite treat.

Chocolate cherry star cakes.

"I must tell Bloop,"
said Louie.
"He LOVES making cakes."

Bloop always sits
in the shopping bag
for safe keeping.
But this time, when Louie
reached into the bag,
he felt something strange.

"What's THIS!"
cried Louie.
"THIS isn't Bloop!"

It wasn't a Thing
with a String.
It was a stringless
Horsey thing.
And when he pressed
its nose it went DIP-DOP.

"Hmmm," said Louie's mum.
"I think we've got the wrong shopping."

So back they went.
Back to the supermarket
on Andromeda 9 on the
far side of the Alpha Galaxy.

"Will we find Bloop?" asked Louie.
"I hope so," replied Louie's mum
as she helped him into his rocket back pack.

"Bloop Rescue ready to GO!"
And off they whooshed.

Louie looked in the baskets
and trolleys as they whizzed by.
"What have you lost?" asked
a lady with long, stripy legs.
Louie told her about Bloop,
the Thing with a String.
"We've come to find him," he said.

The lady with long, stripy legs told
her friend with a curly-wurly snozzle
who told a man with a big, spotty belly.

"We'll help you!" they said.

The lady with long stripy legs looked on the high shelves.

Her friend with the curly-wurly snozzle looked on the low shelves. And the man with the big, spotty belly thought he'd found Bloop . . .

. . . but it was just a long string of spaghetti.

Soon everyone in the supermarket
was looking for Bloop.
They looked in the fruit . . .

under the vegetables . . .
behind the wobbly jellies . . .
through the jammy doughnuts . . .
and along the delicatessen counter.

They looked from the sausages at one end, to the stinky cheeses at the other.

But Bloop was nowhere to be found. "Where can he be?" sighed Louie. Then he saw something . . .

. . . it was very long and very wiggly and it went right round the corner to the tinned tomatoes.

Louie followed it and then pulled the string . . .

Crash!

With a loud clatter,
all the tomato tins
tumbled to the floor.

There, to Louie's surprise, was somebody else.

Her name was Venus. And she was looking for HER cuddliest, most precious toy.

"It's Horsey Dorsey!"
cried Venus.
And, just to make sure,
she pressed his nose.

She pressed it gently.

"DIP-DOP!"
went Horsey Dorsey.
Venus gave Horsey Dorsey
the BIGGEST cuddle and
then gave something to Louie.

Dip-Dop

"It's Bloop!" cried Louie.
And, just to make sure,
he pulled the string.
He pulled it as far
as it would go.

"BLOOP!" went Bloop. Louie gave Bloop the BIGGEST cuddle and everyone in the supermarket cheered.

Now they could swap shopping and leave the supermarket on Andromeda 9 on the far side of the Alpha Galaxy.

Louie and Bloop could go home to make their favourite
treat. **Chocolate** cherry star cakes.

And they had two new friends to help them.
"BLOOP!" went Bloop.
He LOVES making cakes.

C2 03:15

C1 03:17

C7 03:24

C5 03:02

C6 02:41

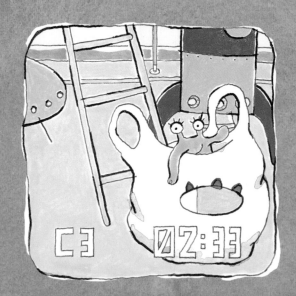

C3 02:33

C3   02:50

C6   02:41

C2   03:16

C4   03:03

C5   02:51

C8   03:19

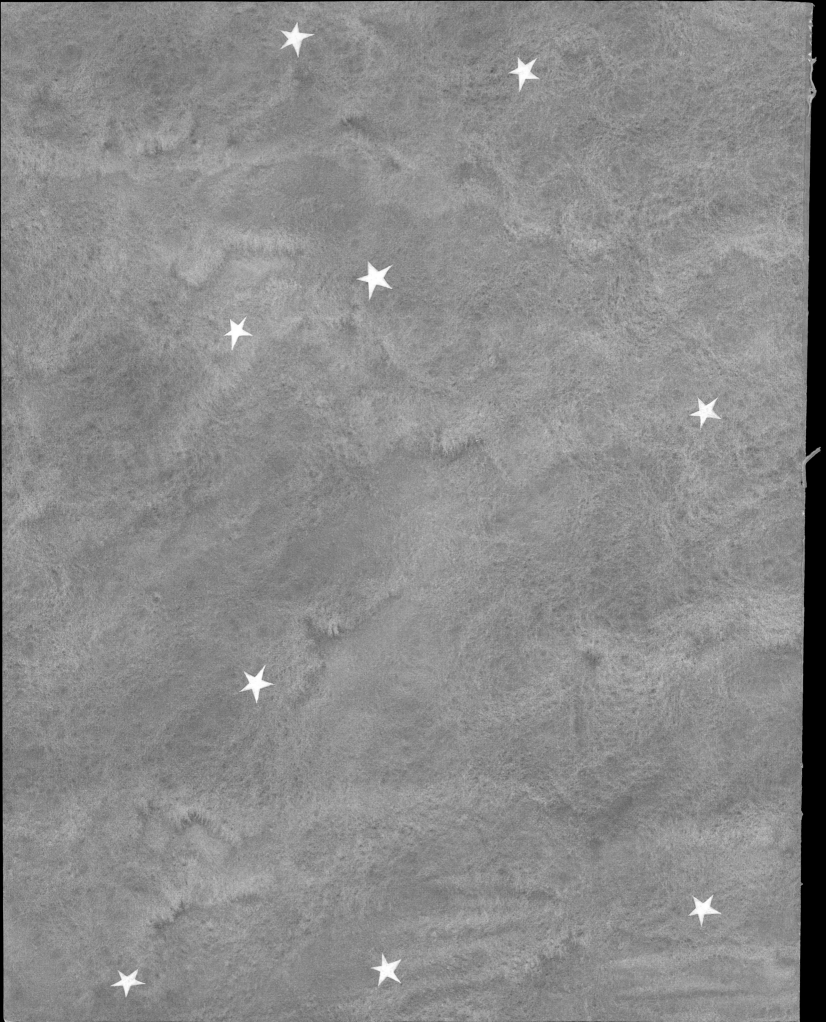